Dear

Have you ever done something that you knew you weren't supposed to do it until you had already done it? Well, that's what happened to Andy and me. We learned how important it is to obey our moms and dads and how important it is to keep promises.

I hope you learn as much as Andy and I did!

Sincerely,
Joey

THE ADVENTURES OF Andy Ant™
The Swimming Hole Disaster

Created by Lawrence W. O'Nan
Written by Gerald D. O'Nan
Illustrated by Norman McGary

Dedicated to Jessica Leigh O'Nan

Tyndale House Publishers, Inc.
Wheaton, Illinois

First printing, August 1988. ISBN 0-8423-0313-8. Text and illustrations © 1988 by Andy Ant Productions. Andy Ant is a trademark of Andy Ant Productions, Inc. All rights reserved. Printed by Zrinski, Yugoslavia.

It was a hot summer afternoon. As I walked outside, I was sure glad that my mom had said I could wait until evening to finish pulling the weeds in the garden. I walked over to the crack in the sidewalk and looked in. I wanted to see if Andy Ant was in his room.

I bent over and whispered, "Andy, are you in there?" I had to whisper because Mr. Davis, our next-door neighbor, was out in his yard. If he heard me, he might think I was talking to the sidewalk. And I didn't want to have to explain what I was really doing. Most grown-ups would think talking to ants was even stranger than talking to the sidewalk!

There was no answer from Andy, so I thought to myself, *Where would an ant go on a day like this?* Well, I knew where *I* would be if my mom hadn't told me not to leave the yard. I'd be over at the swimming pool. And I knew Andy and I think a lot alike, even though he's a philosopher—that's what we call Andy because he has deep thoughts and understands how important it is to do things right—and I'm just what he calls "a regular kid." So maybe he was at his swimming hole.

I walked over to the ant swimming hole. It's where the gutter dips along the curb in front of my house. Sure enough, there was Andy. He was lying on his beach towel, sleeping. "Hey, Andy, what are you doing?" I asked as I kneeled down.

Andy slowly opened his eyes. "Hi, Joey," he said with a smile. "I'm just waiting for Parker to come out so I can go swimming."

Parker is Andy's older brother, a real practical kind of ant. "Why do you have to wait for Parker?" I asked Andy. "The water isn't going to be any warmer if Parker is here, is it?"

Andy just made a face at me. "I have to wait for Parker because my dad said to. You see, Parker is a better swimmer than I am. And my dad says I can't go swimming without Parker."

"Oh, you're a great swimmer," I said. "What could possibly happen?"

"Well, I don't know . . . ," Andy started.

"You do whatever you want," I said, "but I don't think your dad realizes you're getting old enough to do nearly anything you want."

At first, Andy looked a little unsure. But as I talked he became more confident that nothing could go wrong. Besides, it was a hot day and the water would feel great! Then I thought of something.

"Andy," I said, "I can watch you. My mom said I couldn't leave the yard, so I'll be here. You'll be perfectly safe!" Andy brightened up.

"I guess you're right, Joey. There isn't really any reason to wait. And the sun is so hot!" With that, Andy jumped up from his beach towel and headed for the diving board. It wasn't a real diving board, it was an old branch that hung over the curb. But it worked for the ants.

With as much grace and poise as a fourth-grade ant could muster, Andy did a "gliding ant" dive into the water. Actually, a "gliding ant" dive is a lot like a swan dive. But Andy thinks swans eat ants, so we don't use that name.

Andy came to the surface of the water and hollered, "Wow, Joey, the water is great! Too bad the gutter isn't bigger so you could come in too!"

I sat on the edge of the curb, watching Andy as he swam and did some other dives. Every time he looked at me, he would tell me how nice the water was.

The sun was getting hotter and hotter, and I'd had just about enough of Andy saying how great the water was. Then I noticed some kids up the street gathering around a fire hydrant. *Wow,* I thought, *wouldn't it be great if they were going to turn it on?* Sure enough, that's what the firemen were getting ready to do.

By now, Andy had gotten tired of swimming and had crawled up on a floating leaf. He looked like he was asleep again, so I decided not to bother him. I would just run up the street for a while to play in the water from the hydrant.

I got there just as water shot out of the hydrant. It felt really good! Boy, what fun on a hot summer day! I turned to look back down the street, and I froze in horror.

A wall of water was rushing down the gutter, right toward Andy's swimming hole! I was sure that Andy was still fast asleep on the leaf. If he didn't wake up and get out of the swimming hole before the water hit, he would be washed right down the storm sewer drain! I ran toward him, yelling, "Andy! Andy!"

As I got closer I saw Andy on the leaf, sleeping away. "Andy! Wake up!" I screamed at the top of my lungs. Our neighbor, Mr. Davis, looked all around to see who I was yelling at. I knew I would have some explaining to do later, but I didn't care. The important thing was to warn Andy.

But it was too late. The wall of water hit the swimming hole, and Andy was on a one-way trip to the storm sewer.

"Andy! Andy!" I continued to yell. Just as the leaf was about to be washed down the drain, Andy woke up. Seeing what was about to happen, he grabbed the edge of the leaf and looked back at me. The last words I heard him say were, "Get Parker, quick!"

And then he was gone.

I froze again as I watched the water run into the drain. My legs felt like jelly and I thought I was going to be sick. But I had to go find Parker. I charged down the sidewalk toward Andy's house and almost stepped on Parker. He was loaded down with his radio and umbrella over one shoulder, and a lounge chair and jug of lemonade over the other one. I was surprised he could even stand up. "Hey, slow down, Joey," he said, dropping his stuff all over the sidewalk. "One wrong step and you would have had squashed ant for supper."

"Oh, Parker," I gasped, "you've got to come to the swimming hole, fast!"

"Sure, sure, I'm coming," he said as he leaned over to pick his stuff up. "But it's going to take me a few minutes to get all my gear down there."

"But Parker," I pleaded, "Andy's in trouble! He went in swimming 'cause I said I'd watch him and I wasn't supposed to leave the yard and the fire hydrant was on so I went up the block to play in it and the water washed Andy down the storm sewer!" I said it all so fast I wasn't sure Parker understood. But he caught the most important part.

"Did you say Andy was washed down the storm sewer?" he asked, dropping his gear all over the sidewalk again.

"Uh huh," I said, wiping away a tear.

"Well, let's go!" Parker yelled as he hopped on my right sneaker. And we ran back down the sidewalk.

When we got to the gutter, Parker took one look at the
water gushing down the drain and said, "Oh no! If only I
hadn't taken so much time to find all my gear! We'd better go get my dad!"

We ran over to the vacant lot where Mr. Ant worked,
building ant condominiums. Parker jumped off my shoe
and ran to find his dad. When his dad heard what had
happened to Andy, he rounded up several of

his best workers. They all got on my sneakers and we nearly flew back to the gutter in front of my house.

While Andy's dad was deciding what to do, the firemen up the street turned off the hydrant, and the gush of water became a trickle. Just as Mr. Ant was moving things into action, a little ant head popped up from the edge of the storm sewer grate. It was Andy!

"Andy!" we all yelled, "You're safe!"

"Yeah," he said with a smile as his dad ran over to wrap him in a towel and hug him. "But I thought I was a goner for sure. I was really glad I was on the leaf, 'cause it got stuck in the grate. And I was able to get off and hold onto the bottom side of the grate until the water stopped. Just think, I might have been floating somewhere under the city of Grand Ant by now. Maybe I wouldn't even have been floating at all. . . ."

"You're right, Andy," said Mr. Ant. "This could have been much worse. But it wouldn't have happened if you'd waited for Parker like I told you to." Andy looked down at the ground and I felt pretty bad about talking him into going swimming.

While Mr. Ant helped Andy dry off, I decided I should explain that it wasn't all Andy's fault. Mr. Ant listened as I told him what had happened. And Parker even apologized for taking so long to find his gear.

Since everything seemed to be under control, Mr. Ant and his workers went back to the vacant lot. But before he left, he told Andy and Parker that there would be a "serious talk" at their house that evening.

As Parker walked back up the sidewalk to pick up his scattered gear, Andy and I sat down on the curb.

"Boy," he said, "I just hate it when Dad says we're going to have a 'serious talk.' I'd rather he'd spank me so it would be over faster."

Then he looked at me. "But you know, Joey," he said in his philosopher's voice, "we were both wrong in what we did today. I should have obeyed my dad and not gone swimming without Parker. I've even heard your mom say that God wants us to obey our parents. And you should have stayed there to watch me like you promised you would."

"I'm really sorry, Andy," I said, afraid I was going to cry again.

"I know you are," Andy said, still talking in that low, serious voice.

Just then I heard my mother call from the front door. "Joseph Tyler Johnson," she said to me, "where have you been? I thought I told you not to leave the yard! You come in here right now. I think we need to have a little talk about obeying your parents!"

"Uh, coming, Mom," I said, then I looked down at Andy and shrugged. "I guess I'll get to learn two lessons today instead of one."

He just smiled and said, "Well, be sure you listen close. Your mom's pretty smart, for a person."

"I will, Andy, I promise," I said, getting up to go inside.

Later, as I got ready for bed, I thought about the day. I was glad everything had turned out all right. And I was really glad Andy was safe. I remembered the look on his face as the leaf had been washed away . . . then I smiled.

"One thing's for sure," I said with a little laugh. "With Andy for a friend, this summer will never be boring!" Then I hurried to get ready for bed, looking forward to tomorrow and my next adventure with Andy Ant.

Dad

Mom

Angelica

Parker

Uncle Andrew

Dickter

your Friend,
Andy

Andy's Family (Me)